Rebecca Donnelly   illustrated by **Misa Saburi**

CATS ARE A LIQUID

GODWINBOOKS

Henry Holt and Company · New York

Cats fill.

Cats spill.

Cats flow downhill.

Cats tip.

Cats drip.

DO NOT ENTER

WOOF WEEK

Cats
grip,
snip,
rip.

Cats are a liquid

Cats slop.

Cats plop.

**Cats
drizzle,
slosh,
flop.**

Cats train, aim, maim.

Cats are a liquid

except when they're not.

Cats spout.

Cat drought.

Cat flash flood.

Drench.

Sprout.

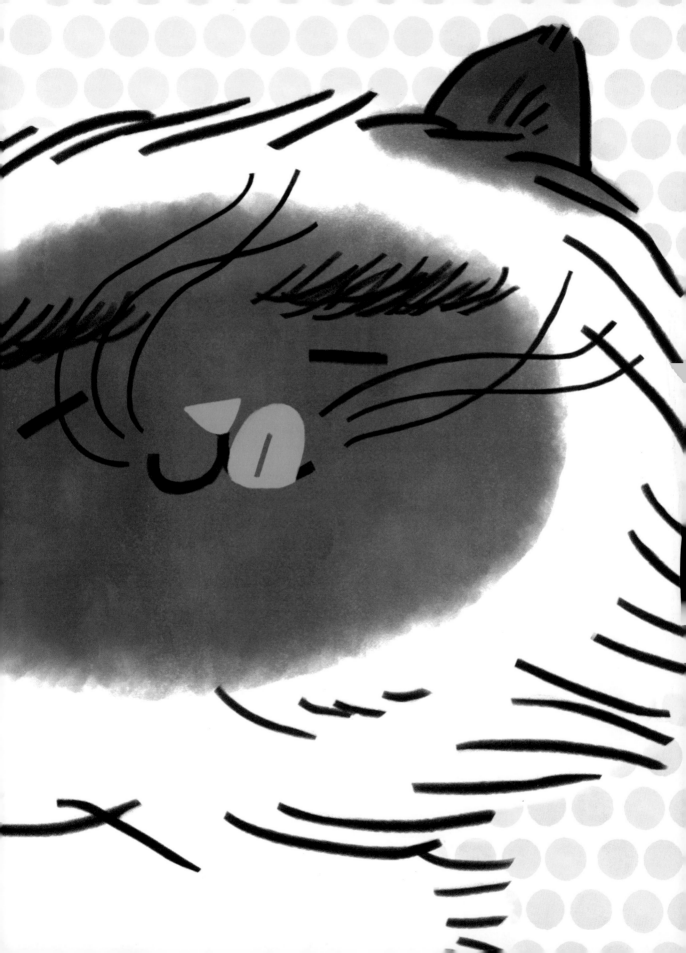

A cat's not a liquid

except when it is.

Roll,

crest,

ripple,

fizz.

Blanket.

Nap.

Cats are clouds
in the atmosphere.

Evaporate.

Precipitate.

Are cats a liquid?

Matter is the stuff all around you. Your clothes, your food, and your cat are all made of matter. There are many states of matter. The most common are solid, liquid, and gas. You can see examples of all three in everyday life. You can even see matter change from one state to another.

Think about the water that comes out of your kitchen faucet. That's a liquid. If you put water into an ice cube tray and freeze it, soon you'll have ice, a solid. If you melt the ice, you're back to liquid water. Put the water in a pot and boil it on the stove (with a grown-up!), and the steam you see is a gas. But they're all the same chemical: H_2O.

Does a cat really act like a liquid? It's a science joke, based on the way cats seem to fill up any container they squeeze themselves into. If you pour water into a tall, thin glass, it takes that shape. If you pour it into a wide bowl, it takes the shape of the bowl. Solids behave differently. If you put a solid, like an ice cube, into a cup or a bowl, it holds its shape (until it melts, of course).

A quick look on the internet will show you that cats can fit themselves into bowls, cups, pans, boxes, and many other containers, and their bodies seem to fill the container in the same way a liquid does.

That is, unless you're trying to put them in a bathtub—and then they're solid, rigid, and extremely hard to handle!

Learn more about states of matter

James, Emily. *The Simple Science of Matter.* Capstone Press: North Mankato, 2018.

Sjonger, Rebecca. *Changing Matter in My Makerspace.* Crabtree Publishing: New York, 2018.

Read about the scientific paper that started it all

slate.com/technology/2017/11/how-assessing-if-a-cat-is-a-liquid-advanced-science.html

Activity

Are cats liquid or solid . . . or oobleck?

There really is something that can act like a solid or a liquid without going through a phase change like melting or boiling: oobleck! The name comes from a Dr. Seuss book, *Bartholomew and the Oobleck,* but it's a real substance you can make at home.

Ingredients

1 cup water

1 to 2 cups cornstarch

Directions

Mix the cornstarch and water with a wooden spoon in a large bowl. You might need to add more water or cornstarch to get the right consistency. Your oobleck should be thick enough to be picked up in a chunk but liquid enough to run back through your fingers into the bowl.

Try hitting the surface of your oobleck, digging into it with a spoon, or sculpting something with it. How does it behave? What else can you do with it?

When you're done

Never pour oobleck down the sink! Just like a cat, it can act like a solid at the wrong time, and you don't want solid cornstarch clogging up your pipes. Scrape it into the trash and rinse your bowl with a lot of water.

Find out more about oobleck

scientificamerican.com/article/oobleck-bring-science-home

legacy.mos.org/discoverycenter/aotm/2009/04

To Sara, in all her states —R. D.

To all cats waiting to be adopted —M. S.

Henry Holt and Company, *Publishers since 1866*
Henry Holt® is a registered trademark of Macmillan Publishing Group, LLC
120 Broadway, New York, NY 10271 • mackids.com

Library of Congress Cataloging-in-Publication Data
Names: Donnelly, Rebecca, author. | Saburi, Misa, illustrator.
Title: Cats are a liquid / Rebecca Donnelly ; illustrated by Misa Saburi.
Description: First edition. | New York : Henry Holt and Company, 2019. | "Godwin Books." | Summary:
Illustrations and simple, rhyming text pay tribute to cats and their resemblance to a liquid. Includes
facts about states of matter and directions for making oobleck. | Includes bibliographical references.
Identifiers: LCCN 2019002537 | ISBN 9781250206596 (hardcover)
Subjects: | CYAC: Stories in rhyme. | Cats–Fiction. | Matter–Properties–Fiction. | Humorous stories.
Classification: LCC PZ8.3.D7239 Cat 2019 | DDC [E]–dc23
LC record available at https://lccn.loc.gov/2019002537

Our books may be purchased in bulk for promotional, educational, or business use.
Please contact your local bookseller or the Macmillan Corporate and Premium Sales Department
at (800) 221-7945 ext. 5442 or by email at MacmillanSpecialMarkets@macmillan.com.

First edition, 2019 / Design by Liz Dresner
All illustrations were drawn in Adobe Photoshop.
Printed in China by RR Donnelley Asia Printing Solutions Ltd., Dongguan City, Guangdong Province

1 3 5 7 9 10 8 6 4 2